nickelodeon

# PAW PATROL™

# PIT CREW PUPS

PaRragon

Bath · New York · Cologne · Melbourne · Delhi
Hong Kong · Shenzhen · Singapore

This edition published by Parragon Books Ltd in 2016

Parragon Books Ltd
Chartist House
15–17 Trim Street
Bath BA1 1HA, UK
www.parragon.com

By Kristen Depken
Based on the teleplay "Pups Pit Crew" by Franklin Young
Illustrated by MJ Illustrations

ISBN 978-1-4748-5703-1

Printed in China

**This book belongs to**

_____

_____

It was a beautiful day in Adventure Bay. Alex Porter went to visit his grandpa. He had something special to show him.

"Hey, Grandpa," said Alex. "Check out what I made from this old restaurant stuff. It's a Super Trike!"

The trike was great. It had a seat made from a wooden vegetable crate and the brake was a pizza paddle – the kind that Alex's grandpa uses to pull pizzas out of the oven.

"Nice!" said Grandpa. "You used lots of tape."
"Just like you taught me," Alex grinned. "Watch!"
He grabbed the handlebars, jumped into the seat
and pushed off.

The trike rolled over a bump. *BANG!* The back
wheels fell off. *CLANG!* The front wheel bounced away.
*CRASH!* The handlebars came apart. Alex was left sitting
in a vegetable crate!

"My Super Trike is ruined," he sighed.

Alex's grandpa pulled out his mobile phone. "I know
who can help," he smiled.

Ryder was fixing the wheel of his all-terrain-vehicle when the call came through.

"Alex could use some help," said Mr Porter. "I know you're pretty handy with gadgets and vehicles, Ryder."

"Tell him we're on our way!" said Ryder. "PAW Patrol, let's roll!"

When there's trouble in Adventure Bay, PAW Patrol is always ready for action! Ryder and the pups jumped in their trucks and raced to the rescue.

The PAW Patrol was on the case in no time.
Ryder helped Alex pick up his broken trike from
the road, while Chase slowed down the cars.

The team took the broken trike back to the Lookout garage. Rocky and Ryder got to work, fixing it up and putting the wheels back on with bolts.

Rocky gave Ryder a pair of pedals from his recycling bin. "Don't lose it, reuse it!" said Rocky.

"Just remember to keep your feet on the pedals at all times," Ryder explained.

The new Super Trike was even better than before!
Alex couldn't wait to try it out.

"Come on, Ryder," yelled Alex. "Let's race!"

Ryder helped Alex put his helmet on. "You need
to get used to your vehicle first," he replied. "Let's
take a slow drive down the Lookout driveway."

But Alex wasn't listening. He raced straight out
of the garage and down the driveway. *ZOOM!*
Ryder, Chase and Rocky ran after the trike, but it
went faster and faster until they couldn't keep up!

Ryder and the pups
jumped in their trucks
and followed Alex down
the hill.

"Alex!" called Ryder.
"Slow down!"

But Alex was having too much fun. "Wheeeee! Look at me go!" he shouted.

He kicked his feet in the air and zoomed down the hill. Soon, Alex was out of control.

"Help," he cried. "I can't get my feet back on the pedals – they're turning too fast!"

Ryder gasped. Alex was heading towards a busy street. Cars and lorries were speeding along the main road at the bottom of the driveway.

"Chase," Ryder called into his helmet mike, "secure the traffic!"

Chase skidded his truck to a stop, switched on his flashing lights and signalled to the traffic.

The cars and lorries waited at the junction and Alex and Ryder zipped safely by. But Alex's trike was still out of control. PAW Patrol had to slow him down, fast!

Skye hovered overhead in her helicopter.

"Skye," radioed Ryder, "can you hook Alex's trike?"

"You got it, Ryder," Skye barked, flying low over the bridge. She swung her hook down and grabbed the back of the Super Trike. The trike slowed down to a stop. Alex was safe!

Ryder and the pups cheered. "Great work, Skye!"

Alex climbed safely out of his trike. "Thanks, Skye!"
he said, giving her a wave.
Ryder and the pups hurried over to their friend.

"I'm sorry," Alex whispered. "If I'd started slowly, like you said, this wouldn't have happened."

"That's okay," smiled Ryder, "but whenever you try something new, you have to start out slowly."

Alex nodded. "Thanks, PAW Patrol! You saved me and my Super Trike!"

Ryder decided to take
everyone to the lemonade stand.
"Let's race on over!" said Alex,
running towards his trike.
Skye and Rocky shook their heads.
"Oops!" said Alex. "I mean roll
on over."

The PAW Patrol crew jumped in their trucks. Together, they showed Alex how to ride the Super Trike gently and safely along the road.

When they got to the lemonade stand, Ryder had a surprise for Alex.

"You've earned the safe driving cup," he beamed.

Ryder handed Alex a gold trophy full of ice cream. It was his own yummy, special gift from the PAW Patrol!